TREASURES *of* CHILDHOOD

HATTIE'S FARAWAY FAMILY

BOOK 2 OF
THE HATTIE COLLECTION

Marie Hibma Frost

PUBLISHING

Colorado Springs, Colorado

Hattie's Faraway Family

Copyright © 1994 by Marie Hibma Frost
All rights reserved. International copyright secured.

Library of Congress Cataloging-in-Publication Date
Frost, Marie
            Hattie's faraway family/ by Marie Hibma Frost.
                    p.   cm. — (Hattie series : 2)
            Summary: Hattie's cousin Katrina, who lives in Chicago, comes to
visit the farm after her parents are killed in an accident.
            ISBN 1-56179-215-2
            [1. Farm life—Fiction. 2. Cousins—Fiction.I. Title.
II. Series: Frost, Marie.   Hattie   series; 2.
    PZ7. F9216Hav 1994
    [Fic]—dc20   94-10281
                                                            CIP
                                                            AC

Published by Focus on the Family Publishing
Colorado Springs, Colorado 80995
Distributed by Word Books, Dallas, Texas

Editor: Etta Wilson
Interior design: Harriette Bateman
Interior illustration: Buford Winfrey
Cover design: Jeff Stoddard
Cover illustration: Randy Nelson

Printed in the United States of America
94 95 96 97 98 99/10 9 8 7 6 5 4 3 2 1

To Eugene
for his patience while I wrote these books.

Some Words You May Need to Know

praten . . . . .idle talk or chatter

streusel . . . . . .a crumbly mixture of sugar,
             flour, and butter that is used
             as topping for cakes

ya . . . . .yes

fanka . . . . . . .girl

liefheid . . . . . .sweetheart

soup'n brie . . .a soup-like mixture of milk
             and cheese, sometimes eaten
             with syrup

CONTENTS

Chapter 1

Hattie's Cousin Comes to Visit

*T*oday was the day! Hattie ran down the stairs. The school year was finished, and her cousin Katrina from Chicago was coming to visit the Hart farm.

Mom was making cinnamon streusel in the kitchen when Hattie came racing in.

"Oh, please! Oh, please! May I go with Dad to pick up Katrina at the train depot?" begged Hattie. She hopped up and down with excitement.

"*Ya, ya,*" laughed Mom. "But you could let Dad finish his lunch first."

Hattie sat down at the dining table and watched her father as he ate. Oh, how she wished he would hurry! He just kept chewing!

She wondered what would happen if they got to the depot late and Katrina was already there, waiting. She would think they had forgotten about her. She might even be afraid, standing there alone in a strange place. The Harts shouldn't leave her waiting on a train platform!

At last, Dad finished his meal and got up. "I'll go out and hitch up the wagon," he told Hattie. "You wait for me in front."

"Why aren't you using the car?" Hattie asked.

"Now, Hattie, you know I only drive the car to church. Besides, the wagon will work better to carry Katrina's trunk."

Following Dad out the kitchen door, Hattie hopped off the porch and stood waiting. Her ears strained for the first sound of the creaking wagon wheels and the clop, clop of the horses' hoofs. At last he came, sitting tall in the driver's seat. He reached down to help Hattie climb up into the wagon. Then he slapped the reins sharply and the horses slowly trotted down the driveway.

"Do you think Katrina will like me?" she asked as Dad turned the wagon out onto the road toward town. "She's just my age, you know."

"How can she help but like you?" teased Dad.

"But, Dad! She's been living in Chicago, where there are lots and lots of things to do. She might be very bored, visiting here with us."

Dad laughed. "With the Harts, things are never boring," he said, giving his daughter a grin. "What bit of mischief one of you doesn't think of doing, the others will."

Hattie kept chattering away, and her father kept nodding in agreement, and the horses kept clop-clopping toward town. At last they heard a train whistle in the distance. As they neared the tracks, Dad slowed the horses to a walk.

They stopped just as the train came huffing and puffing into the station. The noise made the horses nervous, and Dad had to hold the reins tightly to keep them from running away.

The passengers began to climb down from the train to the platform. Hattie saw Katrina right away. She was smaller than Hattie, but she had the same blue eyes and blond hair. She was wearing a beautiful hat and dress. They looked like something Hattie had seen on the cover of the Sears & Roebuck catalog!

Dad nudged Hattie. "Aren't you going to greet your cousin?" he asked his daughter.

Hattie forgot about her dress and began waving wildly. "Katrina! Katrina! We're over here!" Hattie jumped down from the wagon and ran to meet Katrina. "Let me help you with your suitcases."

The two girls walked toward the wagon, Katrina following Hattie. So far, Katrina had not said a word, but when they reached the wagon, Katrina suddenly found her voice. She looked at the horses. She looked at the wagon. She frowned.

"I am not climbing up into that wagon," Katrina

"Katrina! Katrina! We're over here!"

announced, a stubborn look on her face. "It doesn't have a top. If it rains, I'll get my new hat all wet. And even if it doesn't rain, I'll still ruin my clothes sitting on that board in that old wagon." As she finished, she stomped her foot.

Hattie didn't know what Dad would do, but she did know he wouldn't put up with nonsense.

"Hold the horses for a minute, Hattie," Dad said. Hattie did as she was asked. Dad got down from the wagon, picked up Katrina, and placed her firmly on the seat. He tossed her suitcases in the back of the wagon. Then he climbed back up, took the reins, and helped Hattie up. Katrina, a frown on her face, sat stiffly between Hattie and her father as he turned the wagon around to begin the trip home.

Hattie had to think of something to say. She had so looked forward to Katrina's visit. Now here Katrina was, but she wasn't at all what Hattie had imagined.

"I'm glad you're here," Hattie said, carefully choosing her words. "We can do lots of things."

"There's nothing to do on a dirty old farm," said Katrina.

"Oh, yes, there is!" said Hattie. "We have chickens and cows and horses and a big, big garden."

Katrina wrinkled her nose. "That all sounds like work. I'd rather play."

Hattie suddenly remembered that Katrina didn't have any brothers and sisters to play with. Hattie felt very sorry for Katrina. Hattie would have to be very patient, but she was sure once they got to know each other, Katrina would want to be her friend after all.

When Dad drove the horses into the farmyard, all the Hart family came out to greet Katrina. Katrina's eyes grew big. There were Kathryn, Pierce, Clarence, Leona, and Mom holding little Ervin. Everyone wanted to hug her, talk to her, and look at her. She hadn't known she had so many cousins!

Mom had made a special meal in honor of Katrina's arrival. The family sat down at the table, and Dad began to read from the Bible. When he finished, Hattie glanced over at Katrina. She was amazed to see her cousin slumped in her chair—asleep! Dad got up and lifted Katrina onto his shoulder.

"Poor little *fanka*," whispered Dad, carrying her up the stairs to bed.

"Maybe she's tired from her trip on the train," said Hattie's older sister Kathryn.

Hattie looked from her mother to her sister. *Maybe, maybe not*, she thought.

Two Cowgirls

*T*he next morning after everyone had eaten breakfast, Hattie invited Katrina to go outside and walk around the farm. First they went to the chicken house where Hattie showed Katrina the hens sitting on eggs, waiting for their baby chicks to hatch. Katrina looked at the chickens, then looked at the eggs. Then she reached out and grabbed one of the eggs and broke it!

"Why did you do that?" demanded Hattie.

"I wanted to see the baby chicken you said was inside," Katrina replied.

"When it's time for them to come out, I'll show you, but don't go breaking any more eggs!" Hattie was angry. "There won't be any baby chickens in the eggs for some time," she explained.

Hattie led the way to the cow barn, where the cows were standing in their little stalls, waiting to be milked.

"Can we ride them?" Katrina asked, looking at

these strange animals with interest.

"We ride horses, not cows," Hattie said.

"They look big enough to ride," said Katrina. "Why can't we ride them?"

Hattie looked at the cows. It was a good question. Why couldn't they ride them? No one had ever told Hattie that she couldn't ride a cow. It might be fun! As if reading Hattie's mind, Katrina hopped onto the back of the nearest cow. Not to be outdone, Hattie jumped up on Dandelion, a cow she knew was gentle.

"I'm in the rodeo," yelled Katrina, waving one arm up in the air, pretending she was roping a bull. "I have a book at home with a picture of a cowboy, and he looks just like this!"

"I'm a princess, sitting on a throne chair on top of an elegant Indian elephant all covered with jewels," declared Hattie. "I saw a picture like that in a book. I'm wearing a crown with diamonds and there are sparkling spangles all over my dress."

Suddenly, a voice stopped their pretend game.

"What are you girls doing up on those cows?" yelled Pierce, who had come into the barn to do the milking. "Wait till Dad hears about this one. The cows are so upset, they probably won't give any milk!"

"Oh, please, Pierce, don't tell Dad," begged Hattie, as she slid off the back of Dandelion.

"Help me!" Katrina called out, holding tight to the cow's neck. "I'm afraid to get down!"

"I've a notion to leave you here," Pierce said, as he helped Katrina down. "Don't let me ever catch you doing that again," he scolded the girls as they ran out of the barn.

Next Hattie led the way to the horse stable. "If we can't ride cows, will you show me how to ride a horse?" asked Katrina.

"I'm not allowed to ride any horses except old Betsy. If you do what I tell you, I'll show you how to ride her," Hattie offered.

"Oh, goody!" said Katrina, clapping her hands excitedly. "That sounds like fun!"

Hattie wished Dad were there so she could ask permission, but he had been in the fields since very early that morning. And anyway, she was allowed to ride Betsy. It should be all right for Katrina to try.

Pierce agreed to saddle the old mare for the two girls. Then he left Hattie to show Katrina how to mount the horse.

"Stand on the horse's left side," Hattie said, "never the right side. Now grab the saddle horn with your left hand and put your left foot in the stirrup so it won't jiggle. Then give a little jump and throw your right leg over the saddle."

Hattie demonstrated several times, then she let Katrina try. It wasn't easy for Katrina, but Betsy stood patiently. After a few tries, Katrina finally managed to pull herself upright on top of the horse. Hattie gave her the reins.

"Now don't go yelling or anything," warned Hattie. "You don't want to scare Betsy. Just nudge her gently with your knees and she'll start to walk."

Katrina did as Hattie said and Betsy slowly moved forward. Sitting straight in the saddle, Katrina bobbed up and down as Betsy walked calmly around the yard.

"It's easy to ride a horse," Katrina called after a few turns around the yard.

Hattie felt a little nervous about the whole thing. "I think you've had enough riding for one day."

"I've just begun!" Katrina replied stoutly. "I want to go fast and then I'll get off."

Without waiting for Hattie's reply, she kicked the side of the horse and yelled at the top of her lungs, "Giddy-up, giddy-up, old Betsy!"

And Betsy did get going! Around and around the yard she went, like a spinning top, with Katrina hanging on for dear life.

"Stop!" yelled Katrina. She dropped the reins. Betsy began to paw the ground, trying to shake Katrina off her back. "Help me!" screamed Katrina. "I'll be killed!"

Hattie tried to get close to Betsy's head without being stepped on. At last, she was able to reach out, grab the bridle, and stop the horse. Katrina was gasping and looking pale, but trying hard not to show she was frightened.

"Please," she begged in a small voice, "Help me down. I want to go back to the house."

Hattie felt shaky inside as she led Betsy back to the barn. "I don't know about Katrina," she whispered to the horse. "She's more than I bargained for, and we haven't even finished walking around the farm!"

Chapter 3

Up a Tree with Katrina

*H*attie saw the clear blue sky and warm sunlight out the window. Something told her it was time for an adventure.

"It's a good day to go down to the creek," she said to Katrina. "Mom and Dad don't care if we play in the water."

Katrina looked surprised. "What will we do in the creek?" she asked.

"Just wait and see," laughed Hattie. Grabbing Katrina's hand, Hattie pulled her out the door, and the two girls skipped down the path to the water.

All along the creek the green grass bent in the breeze with a few blue violets still peeking out here and there. When the girls got to the edge of the creek, they could hear the water making a soft, singing sound as it bubbled over the rocks.

Hattie loved the beauty of the place, and right away she wanted to make up a poem. Dreamily, she stood on the bank while words came to her lips:

"The grass whispers and the soft wind blows,
And the creek is singing as it flows and flows."

Hattie repeated the poem to Katrina. "It's so beautiful, it makes me want to cry," exclaimed Hattie.

Katrina looked strangely at Hattie.

Suddenly, Hattie's mood changed. The day was too perfect to spend dreaming on the creek bank. "Let's take off our shoes and socks and jump in!" said Hattie.

Katrina obeyed and soon the two girls were ankle-deep in the bubbling creek. The water was warm and the mud felt good squishing between their toes.

Bending over, Katrina peered closely at the water. "I see some tiny fish," she announced.

"I see a water bug skating on the water," said Hattie. The two girls, looking for more marvels in the creek, wandered along the bank until they came to a bridge where a road ran over the creek.

"What's that?" asked Katrina, pointing to something resting high on the bank.

"It's a raft. My brothers made it," said Hattie. "Sometimes they float down the stream on it."

"Can we use it?" asked Katrina.

Hattie hesitated. "I don't know," she said. "It belongs to Pierce and Clarence. I've never been on a raft before, but maybe we could ride a little way on it."

A voice in her head cautioned Hattie. Her ideas were always getting her in trouble, but riding a raft sounded like fun. They climbed the bank and tried to push the raft down toward the water, but it had been pulled high to keep it from floating away. Hattie and Katrina had to push and push to get it into the water. Finally, the two sailors were on their way.

As they floated along, they could tell that the water on the far side of the bridge was much deeper.

"Isn't this divine?" sighed Hattie, lying down flat on her back so that she could look up at the blue sky. "It's pure ecstasy." Hattie was always trying to use big words even though sometimes she didn't know what they meant.

"I'm a princess floating away to fairyland," Hattie imagined. "There is a prince waiting for me in his castle." Back and forth, up and down, the raft gently rocked as it floated downstream. Lost in her dream world, Hattie didn't notice what was happening around her—until Katrina happened to glance at the bank.

"Hattie! Look!" she shrieked.

Something in Katrina's voice made Hattie sit straight up. "It's Blackie!" shouted Hattie. The huge bull was running straight toward them.

Hattie looked around in terror. She knew that Blackie had been known to jump into the creek if he were mad enough.

21

Several feet ahead of the raft, a weeping willow tree grew close to the bank. "Quick!" commanded Hattie. "We have to climb that tree before Blackie gets here." Both girls jumped off the raft into water so deep that it reached their waists.

Grabbing the nearest branch, Hattie started to climb the tree. Blackie was coming at them faster and faster. And Katrina was still in the water!

"Hurry up!" yelled Hattie. "Grab a branch and climb the tree as fast as you can!"

"I've never climbed a tree before," Katrina shouted. "I can't climb high enough!"

"Yes, you can!" commanded Hattie. "You'd better try or Blackie will kill you!"

Hattie grabbed Katrina by the arm and pulled her up to the lowest tree limb. Just then Blackie, snorting and bellowing with rage, came galloping under the tree. Up, up the two girls climbed as Blackie pawed the ground below them with his hoofs. At last Hattie decided they were high enough.

"That was a close call," Hattie said, still shaking with fright. Her voice shook as she told Katrina, "We need to thank God right now for saving our lives."

Hattie started praying earnestly. "Dear God, dear God," she sobbed, "You are very good. We could have been pounded to pieces if it weren't for You. Forgive me for not being wise and for using the raft without asking. Thank You from the bottom of my heart for having planted a tree right where we needed it. Amen."

Katrina and Hattie were so glad to be safe in the tree that it took them a moment to realize they were trapped. Looking down at the snorting, pawing bull, Katrina asked in a small voice, "Will we have to stay here all night?"

"No," replied Hattie, "but we can't get out of this tree until Blackie goes back to the pasture with the other animals."

But Blackie had a mind of his own. He was perfectly happy where he was. He plopped himself down right under the tree where Hattie and Katrina had taken refuge.

"I think he's staying all night!" moaned Katrina.

"I think so too," admitted Hattie in a small voice. After what seemed like hours, they heard the dinner bell calling everyone to the house for supper.

Katrina started to cry loudly. "I just know we'll never be rescued."

"Yes, we will," Hattie told her, sounding braver than she felt. "You just wait and see."

At the far end of the pasture, the girls could hear Pierce calling the cows as he rounded them up for milking. Blackie saw the other animals leaving and decided to join them. He raised his big body and ambled off, forgetting about the two girls he had trapped in the tree. Katrina and Hattie waited until they were positive that he was in the barnyard behind a locked gate.

"Let's go. Let's go!" yelled Hattie. They tumbled out of the tree and ran without stopping to the safety of the house. Mom and Dad didn't know what to say when they saw Hattie and Katrina come running through the door. The girls were dirty and splashed with mud. Both of them had scratches on their arms and legs from their mad scramble up the tree.

"We narrowly escaped death!" Hattie explained in a breathless voice.

Kathryn came into the room. She wasn't impressed. "You have such a wild imagination," she teased. "I'm sure you were not about to die."

"Yes, we were," said Hattie. "You should have been there!"

Mom and Dad were so glad to have Hattie and Katrina safe that they could hardly think about punishing Hattie. "I guess," Dad said at last, "there will be no leaving the house for you two tomorrow until we are certain you can be trusted again."

Hattie knew she had been bad. She had not only put herself in danger, but Katrina as well. Katrina was her guest, and Hattie had almost let her be gored by Blackie!

Why can't I be good? Hattie asked herself sadly. *If I weren't so curious about trying new things, I wouldn't get into so much trouble.* Deep down in her heart, she knew right from wrong, but sometimes the wrong things seemed so much fun!

The more Hattie thought about being good, the more discouraged she felt. Right after supper she decided that she would try to be more like her big sister Kathryn, who never seemed to do anything wrong. In fact, Hattie was quite sure Kathryn had never sinned. *If I can just be as good as Kathryn,* she thought.

The next morning it was time for Katrina to catch the train back home. Hattie hated saying good-by. When Dad drove the wagon up to the front of the house to load Katrina's suitcases, Hattie hugged her tight.

"You're my favorite cousin, Katrina," Hattie said, "and after only two weeks."

"You're my favorite too," said Katrina with a smile. "At least when we have to climb a tree."

"I'm glad you two are friends," Dad said, "even if your ideas were too much for us at times. Come along, Katrina. You don't want to miss the train."

Hattie stood and waved a long time as Katrina rode off on the wagon. *Why can't Kathryn leave instead of Katrina?* Hattie thought. *I wouldn't miss Kathryn one little bit!*

Chapter 4

Hand-me-down Dress

he more Hattie thought about it, the angrier she became! There was no doubt about it—Kathryn was Mom's pet.

When Hattie asked why Kathryn was allowed to stay up late and play checkers with Pierce, Mom explained, "She's older than you are."

When Hattie wanted to know why she sometimes had to do Kathryn's share of the work, Mom would say, "Kathryn isn't feeling well," or "Kathryn isn't as strong and healthy as you."

Hattie was tired of being strong and healthy—and younger than Kathryn. Hattie wanted to be older, but she couldn't. What was even worse was that Hattie had to wear Kathryn's hand-me-down clothes!

That very day, Kathryn had come parading into the kitchen in a new dress Mother had ordered for her from the Sears & Roebuck catalog.

"I love it! I love it!" gushed Kathryn. She danced around the kitchen, swishing the dress's full skirt in front of Hattie.

"It is beautiful," Mom agreed. "It fits so well. We were lucky to order the right size."

Hattie looked at Kathryn strutting around the room in her new blue dress. "I always have to wear Kathryn's old, leftover clothes," Hattie grumbled.

"Not leftover," Mom said lightly, "just outgrown. Kathryn is very careful with her dresses. After she outgrows them there is a lot of wear left in them."

Hattie didn't care how much "wear" was left in Kathryn's clothes. They were hand-me-downs. Everyone who saw Hattie in them knew the clothes had once belonged to Kathryn. Hattie wanted to wear new clothes, clothes that had never belonged to anyone else. *It's not fair*, she thought.

However, when Mom called Kathryn's old clothes "outgrown," it had given Hattie an idea. After she finished her chores, Hattie hurried upstairs to the bedroom she shared with Kathryn and Leona. She took the two dresses that Kathryn had recently handed down to her into the room where Mom kept the sewing machine. Hattie had just learned to sew on the machine, and now she was going to use it on the hated dresses.

I can sew these dresses so they won't fit me, either, she told herself. She turned each dress inside out and made a one-inch seam on each side. Then she cut off the original seams.

"Now this dress is really outgrown," she said, smiling as she held up one of the dresses and admired her handiwork. When she slipped the dress over her head, she could barely get it over her shoulders.

If she didn't wiggle or breathe too deeply, she could still wear it. Soon Mom would realize that these dresses were too small for her. Maybe Mom would order Hattie a new dress from the Sears catalog!

That afternoon, Mom said to Hattie, "The Ladies' Aid Society is meeting today at the Broderick house. Mrs. Broderick asked if you would like to help her serve the refreshments." Hattie had never been asked to do anything like this before. She was overjoyed.

"What shall I wear?" she asked excitedly. "My Sunday dress has a big stain on it. I can't wear that!" Maybe Mom had a new dress hidden in her closet somewhere—something just right for her to wear on this special occasion.

Mom didn't have a new dress tucked away for Hattie. Instead, she suggested, "Why don't you wear one of Kathryn's dresses I just gave you? Either one of them will do nicely."

For a moment, Hattie panicked. She thought of the tight seams those dresses had since she had sewn them, but what else could she do? She would have to wear one. There was no other choice. *If I walk very straight and sit real tall, I can manage,* she told herself.

Mother had so much to do before going to the

meeting that she hardly noticed what Hattie was wearing. When the meeting started, Hattie found herself seated next to Mrs. Brinks and her son Albert. "There was no one to watch him at home," whispered Mrs. Brinks when she saw Hattie glaring at the fidgeting boy.

About twenty ladies had gathered in Mrs. Broderick's parlor before the meeting started. Mrs. Broderick opened the piano, a sign that Mrs. Van Wyke was getting ready to sing. Inwardly, Hattie cringed and wondered if she would soon be suffering from an earache.

"I hope she only sings one song," Hattie whispered to her mother. "She has a wiggle in her voice."

"Shhh!" warned Mom.

When Mrs. Van Wyke finally finished singing, Hattie was careful not to clap. She was afraid Mrs. Van Wyke might be encouraged to sing another song. One was enough!

The next order of business was a debate about how much money the society should send to the Retired Ministers Fund. Once they agreed on an amount, the ladies went on to discuss the starving people in Africa. Hattie was grateful she didn't know any starving people in Africa because she was looking forward to eating her sandwich during refreshment time.

Finally the meeting was over. "Would you like to

pass the cream and sugar on this tray?" Mrs. Broderick asked Hattie kindly. "I know I can trust you not to spill the cream."

Hattie beamed with pride, glad to be trusted with such an important job. Holding the tray carefully, Hattie walked over to Mrs. Brinks and her son. "Would you like cream and sugar?" she asked politely.

Just as she leaned over with the tray, she heard a ripping sound. Horrified, she stood straight up, which caused another ripping sound. Hattie's dress was literally coming apart at the seams.

"You've got a big hole in your dress," announced Albert loudly as he pointed at the torn garment. Hattie's face turned red. *Why couldn't Albert keep his big mouth shut?* As quickly as possible, Hattie put the tray down and ran from the room.

In the hall, she looked down and saw that one whole side of her dress was open. She couldn't go back into that room with a torn dress like that. She grabbed her sweater from a hook on the wall and escaped out the back door, racing for home.

If it weren't for Kathryn, I wouldn't be wearing this old hand-me-down dress, Hattie told herself angrily as she ran for home. *If Mom liked me as much as she likes Kathryn, I would have a new dress of my own. I would be at that meeting right now, eating my sandwich with the ladies.*

31

Hattie couldn't bear to think what they were whispering about her—and all because of Kathryn! Safe in her bedroom, Hattie yanked off the hated dress and stuffed it under her bed. "I'm never going to speak to Kathryn again," Hattie muttered as she put on one of her old dresses.

"Hattie," Mom called when she got home. "Come down here."

Hattie slowly came down the stairs to the kitchen. Her mother and Kathryn were starting to peel potatoes for dinner. Hattie, seeing Kathryn look up at her, turned her face away.

"What happened to make you run away from the meeting?" Mom asked with concern.

"You wouldn't understand!" Hattie said, her lower lip trembling. A tear formed at the corner of one eye and slowly made its way down her cheek.

Pierce, who had come into the kitchen in time to hear Hattie's words, made a face at his younger sister. "Why don't you grow up?" he teased her.

"What do you think I'm trying to do?" demanded Hattie.

"You don't have to be so noisy about it," Kathryn said, going back to her potato peeling.

How dare they! None of them cared about her feelings, about how hurt and embarrassed she was. Hattie grew angrier than ever.

"Mind your own business!" she shouted.

"Nobody loves me," moaned Hattie.

"Listen, young lady," Mom began, her voice full of anger. "If you—"

"Darn! Darn! Darn!" Hattie shouted at the top of her voice. She had never said such a bad word before. Maybe now her family would take notice!

She looked around at their stunned faces. Suddenly, Hattie felt overwhelmed by what she had just done. Sobbing, she ran from the room and threw herself on the sofa. Mom followed and soon the whole story came out.

"Nobody loves me!" moaned Hattie.

"Of course we love you," Mom said gently.

"But you love Kathryn more than you love me," Hattie said, tears streaming down her face.

"No, I don't," said Mom. "I have enough love for both of you."

Could that be possible? Hattie, worn out from crying, stopped sobbing to consider Mom's words. Then another horrible thought popped into Hattie's head.

"Will God send me to hell for saying that awful word?" she asked.

"No," Mom smiled. "He understands." She patted Hattie's hand.

"Thank you," Hattie told Mom. "I will never say that horrible word again. I promise."

Hattie felt better. Mom did love her—maybe almost as much as she loved Kathryn.

Chapter 5

Driving to Worthington

*H*attie needed some money! "When school starts I won't have anything," she said to Mom. "I can't buy anything I need."

Kathryn was listening to the conversation. "Is that *need* or *want*, Hattie?"

"Need," said Hattie as she stamped her foot. "I need a new curling iron since the old one is broken, and some Brilliantine to make my hair shiny, and some red anklets to wear with my new red dress."

"We don't have any extra money right now, Hattie, but Mrs. Lynn down the road needs someone to help her," Mom said. "She'll pay you fifty cents a day."

Fifty cents a day, thought Hattie, and *I'm free almost every Saturday.* She was already thinking of more things she needed. *Let's see, I could get a small bottle of "Evening in Paris" perfume and some peppermint sticks and. . . .*

The following Saturday, Hattie started working for Mrs. Lynn. She only had to work in the afternoons.

Hattie didn't mind washing dishes, making beds, and scrubbing floors. It was almost fun at someone else's house.

The next Saturday Mrs. Lynn said to Hattie, "I wish I knew how to drive my car. I need to go shopping in Worthington and I have no one to drive me there."

"I can drive for you," said Hattie even though she had never driven a car before. But she was ten, going on eleven. Most of the boys drove cars when they were twelve, and Pierce had started driving at ten. She was sure she could do it. She did decide, though, that it wouldn't hurt to practice driving first.

"Mrs. Lynn," asked Hattie, "would you care if I drove your car in the pasture for a little bit? It's different from our car and I want to get the feel of it."

"Of course, you can," said Mrs. Lynn happily. "I'll be getting dressed." She was so glad to have a way to get to Worthington.

"All right. I'll just take the car for a turn around the pasture and then we'll go," Hattie replied.

The car was parked in the yard, and Hattie had no trouble getting it started. The first pedal she pushed made the car go backward. "Oops," said Hattie. "I'll have to remember that's the backup pedal."

She stepped on the second pedal. The car jerked forward and Hattie was on her way. She decided the third pedal must be the brake.

Round and round the pasture she went. "This is

"I can drive for you," said Hattie.

easy," said Hattie. She pulled down on the gas lever to make the car go faster.

As she got near the house, she pushed the third pedal. To her relief, it was the brakes. She rolled to a stop in the yard where Mrs. Lynn was waiting.

"Let's be off," Mrs. Lynn said as she climbed into the passenger seat, and they were on their way.

The town of Worthington was seventeen miles away. The first few miles went fairly well. After lurching around a few corners, they stopped suddenly when Hattie accidently put her foot on the brake pedal instead of the go-ahead pedal. It was hard for Hattie to think about the gas lever and the pedals at the same time. She kept doing something wrong with her foot when she was thinking about her hand, or the other way around.

Mrs. Lynn began to suspect that Hattie did not have a lot of experience. "Maybe you should go a little slower since you aren't used to driving my car," she cautioned Hattie. "And you really should stop for the stop signs."

"You don't have to stop when no other car is coming," said Hattie. Actually, she wanted to stop but she kept forgetting which pedal was the brake.

As they drove along, Mrs. Lynn decided it would be safer not to drive on the main highway where there were likely to be more cars. "Let's take the back road into Worthington. I think it will be easier for you," she said to Hattie.

That was a mistake, as Mrs. Lynn soon discovered. The back road was hilly, and Hattie drove the car wildly down the hills, only to stall as it started up again. She could see Mrs. Lynn was getting more and more nervous.

As they came closer to town, they found themselves on a road that circled Lake Okoboja. In some places the waves were lapping at the roadside.

"Why are you holding the door handle?" asked Hattie.

"Just in case I need to jump out in a hurry," said Mrs. Lynn. "I think I'm going to skip shopping today. Let's turn around and head for home." Mrs. Lynn looked white in the face.

Hattie was a little relieved. At least she wouldn't have to drive in a lot of traffic. She managed to turn the car around and started back to the Lynns.

But Mrs. Lynn had had enough of the hilly back roads. "Let's take the main road home," she said. "It will be easier for you."

All the way home no one spoke. Hattie drove very slowly, hoping Mrs. Lynn would feel better. But as they neared home, Hattie glanced over at her. She was holding the door open and had her foot on the running board.

Finally, they turned in the Lynns' driveway and lurched to a stop. Hattie turned off the ignition. Her fingers were cramped from holding the wheel so tight. Mrs. Lynn got out of the car without saying a word.

It was eight o'clock in the evening as Hattie walked into her yard. The whole family was lined up along the fence in front of the house.

"Thank God, you're alive!" said Dad. "Where have you been?"

"I drove Mrs. Lynn to Worthington, at least, almost to Worthington."

"But, Hattie," Dad exclaimed, "you never drove a car in your life before!"

"I have now," said Hattie confidently. With her feet firmly on the ground again, she felt quite proud of what she had done.

As the family walked back to the house, Hattie heard Dad say to Mom, "God takes care of fools and babies, and Hattie is no baby!"

Chapter 6

Lightning!

*H*attie was in the machine shed, rummaging for things to put in a playhouse she had just made in the corncrib. After her dad had sold the corn, he told her she could use the empty space for the playhouse.

She had carried bucket after bucket of water to scrub the floor, spilling a lot of it on her shoes. Her shoes squished when she walked, but it was worth it! Her playhouse was clean and the fun of furnishing it could begin.

Mom had given her some cracked cups and saucers. She used green leaves when she needed extra plates—for her doll or her imaginary friend Evelyn Series. Her table was a cardboard box with a red cloth over it.

Hanging on the wall of the machine shed, Hattie saw a wicker clothes basket with one broken handle. A tattered rug was hanging over its edge.

There's something I could use for a doll bed, thought Hattie. She made her way over to the basket. *I could use that rug, too*, she thought, *if I cut off the ragged edge.*

When she got closer to the basket, she discovered that it was already claimed. A mother hen spread her wings and clucked, warning Hattie not to disturb her. As the hen fluttered her wings, Hattie caught sight of a small hill of eggs under her.

"Sorry, Mrs. Hen, I didn't know you were there," Hattie apologized. She was excited about her discovery. She hurried to the house to tell Mom.

"I guess we'll have more baby chicks one of these days," Mom said.

"Mrs. Hen was pretty smart to hide her nest where she thought no one could find her," said Hattie. "I can't wait until her little chicks arrive."

"Would you like to have those little chicks for your very own?" asked Mom. "You could be responsible for them and take care of them."

"Oh, Mom, do you really mean it? Would they be all mine?" asked Hattie.

"Yes," Mom said. "They would be all yours."

The next day, the chicks began hatching. Each one slowly pecked its way out of a shell—ten fuzzy little yellow balls that felt like cotton when Hattie gently touched them. She loved the peeping sounds that the chicks made.

As Hattie watched the chicks, she noticed that the quiet peeping had turned to loud cheeping. Worried that her new charges were hungry, Hattie went to Mom for advice.

"They probably are hungry," Mom agreed. "I think we can move them to the chicken yard. Here's a pie tin. You can put some chicken feed in it."

Mom showed Hattie where there was a little, round tin chicken coop with a small domed roof.

"When it's dark, they will go in this little house and then you can slide the door shut," Mom explained. "The chicks will be safe for the night. Each morning, you must be sure to open the door and let them out," Mom warned Hattie. "Otherwise, they will get too hot when the sun shines on the tin roof. They might suffocate."

For the first few days, Hattie took good care of her newly acquired family. She remembered to close the little door each night and open it each morning.

When Saturday came, Mom went to town with Dad to get groceries. "Don't forget to do your chores, children," Mom reminded them. "And Hattie, you be sure to let your chicks out before it gets too warm."

"Yes, Mom," Hattie said, as she waved good-bye to her in the wagon.

Hattie had big plans for the day. The new Sears & Roebuck catalog had just arrived in the mail. Without another thought for the chicks, she took the big catalog upstairs and started looking through the children's clothes section.

"Look at these beautiful clothes," Hattie said to herself. She put her finger on one dress that was as blue as a summer sky. It had pearl buttons down the front and a big bow in the back. *If only I could have this dress to wear to church on Sundays,* she thought. *I would be just as pretty and grownup as Kathryn.*

Hattie licked her fingers to help turn to the pages showing hats. There was one that matched the dress. It was exactly the same color blue, and it had little pink roses around the rim and a big silk ribbon hanging down the back. Hattie danced around the room, pretending she was already wearing the new dress and hat; then she looked down at her high-top shoes.

They will never do, thought Hattie. She flipped the pages until she came to the children's shoes. She found one pair that looked so grownup—patent leather slippers with narrow black straps.

"These will make my feet look very elegant," Hattie decided.

Suddenly the big clock in the parlor struck eleven times.

"Oh, no!" Hattie shrieked. "I forgot to open the little coop!"

She ran down the stairs and out of the house to the chicken yard. The hot summer sun was beating down on the little coop. Quickly she opened the door to let her baby chicks out, but there was no sound. Not one peep!

All the chicks were dead. They had suffocated in

their hot little house, just as mom had warned—and it was Hattie's fault.

"Oh, little chicks! Little chicks! I loved you so," sobbed Hattie. "I didn't mean to do it. Why did you have to die? Even if you are in heaven now, I will miss you so."

Hattie sat next to the little coop and cradled several baby chicks in her apron. She stroked their soft, limp bodies as tears streamed down her cheeks.

"What's wrong, Hattie?" asked Clarence, who had come over to the coop to see the baby chicks.

"They're dead," cried Hattie, pointing to the little chicks. "All dead! What shall I do!"

"You will have to bury them," said Clarence solemnly.

Hattie looked down at the little chicks. Clarence was right. Hattie couldn't hold them forever. Another thought occurred to her: What would Mom and Dad say if they found her sitting here by the chicken coop with her lap full of dead chicks?

"Clarence," Hattie addressed her brother sadly, "will you help me bury them? I'm too sad to do it by myself."

Proud to help his sister, Clarence followed her into the farthest grove of trees.

Hattie found a quiet place under a tree and dug a hole in the soft dirt with her heel. After she laid the chickens' delicate bodies down, Clarence covered them with leaves and branches. The pair walked slowly toward the house. Hattie was so upset, she hardly knew what she had done.

Soon Mom and Dad were back. "It looks like it's going to storm," Mom said as she hurried down from the wagon. "Kathryn, get the clothes off the line before it rains. Hattie, you help her."

Hattie ran to grab the clothes that were whipping and snapping on the line. Dark clouds spread across the sky from the west. They were blacker than any she had ever seen. She could see flashes of lightning and hear the rumble of thunder in the distance.

By the time the clothes were off the line and the girls were in the house, the wind was blowing even harder. Dad came rushing into the kitchen.

"It's going to be a bad one," he warned. "We'd better go to the cellar."

That's all Hattie had to hear. She rushed to her room and got her treasure box and writing tablet and raced down to the cellar—the Harts' place of safety in a storm. Mother and the other children were already there.

Lightning flashed and thunder rumbled. Hattie looked out the high cellar window. Trees were bending in the wind and branches were flying through the air. Even though it was still daytime, the sky was as black as night. Hattie knew she had not been good today. Maybe God wanted to strike her dead right there in her hiding place.

Suddenly there was a blinding flash and the loud pop of an explosion. Hattie grabbed Kathryn's hand and the younger children began to cry. Mom went to peek out the high cellar window.

"Ach! Nick, look!" Mom cried, her voice shaking. "The Bests' barn is on fire. You have to go!"

Hattie had a terrible thought. Was God aiming for their farm and hit Arnold's by mistake? As she huddled with her brothers and sisters in the cellar, tears filled her eyes. She knew she had forgotten the chicks because she wanted to look like Kathryn.

After the storm had cleared and Dad and Pierce returned home, the events of the day still whirled in Hattie's mind. That night she didn't protest when it was time for bed, but she couldn't go to sleep.

"I need to talk to God," Hattie said as she lay in bed that night. "Dear Father, I hope it wasn't my fault that Arnold's barn got hit. Arnold skips church sometimes, and he says mean things sometimes, but I know he will repent—and I will, too."

Hattie finished her prayer. "I repent for daydreaming and not letting my little chicks out of their coop," she said. "Please forgive me. Amen."

When Hattie asked God for forgiveness, she always pictured Jesus' kind face—like the one tacked to the bulletin board at Sunday School. She knew God forgave her that very moment, but she also knew that only part of her job was done. Telling Mom about the chicks would be even harder than telling God.

Right then she got out of bed and went downstairs. Mom was in her bedroom, mending the torn knee of Clarence's pants.

"Mom, I need to tell you something," said Hattie slowly. She looked straight into Mom's eyes.

"Is it about the baby chicks?" asked Mom.

Hattie nodded. "How did you know?" she asked with big tears coming to her eyes.

"I asked Clarence how he tore the knee to his pants, and he told me that it happened when he was burying the chicks."

"Oh, Mom, I am so sorry," Hattie said as she ran to her mother's arms.

"You must learn from these things to do better next time," Mom said as she patted Hattie on the back.

"I will try," Hattie promised. *And I must not be jealous of Kathryn,* she thought.

Chapter 7

A Hot, Hot Day

*T*he summer morning dawned just as hot as the one before. By afternoon, the kitchen was sweltering. Hattie felt as red and hot as the tomatoes she was dipping into scalding water.

Dipping them first into hot water and then into cool water made their tough skins slide off more easily. But that didn't make her standing in the fiery kitchen any easier. She wished she could dip her whole body in the cool water.

"I'm just too hot!" she complained to Kathryn, sweat dripping off her forehead and stinging her eyes. "If I have to peel one more tomato, I'll faint! My fingers feel like prunes, my hair is soaked with sweat, and my back aches from leaning over this pan."

"And," interrupted Kathryn, "this is canning time. You're supposed to be a helper. All you are is a big complainer. Get busy or I'll tell Mom on you. You don't earn your keep."

"Tattletale," muttered Hattie.

As Mom entered the kitchen, she let out a long sigh. "Ya," she said, "the kitchen is too hot anymore.

This is enough work to do for one day."

Hattie bolted for the door before Mom could change her mind or decide that Hattie needed to lie down. What she needed was a breath of cool, fresh air. She was dismayed to find the air outside was just as red-hot and sultry as the air inside.

Standing on the barnyard gate, Hattie saw Pierce leaving to bring the cows home from the pasture. "May I go with Pierce?" Hattie asked Dad, who was repairing some machinery so he could make hay the next day.

"If you don't spook the cows," laughed Dad as he wiped sweat from his forehead. "And don't loiter along the way either. The cows need to be milked before supper time."

With the mess from the tomatoes to be cleaned, Hattie figured supper would be so late she didn't need to hurry. She and Pierce walked slowly down the lane toward the pasture. *No doubt the cows are sweating too*, thought Hattie.

"I'll show you a secret," Pierce offered. "See this bunch of tall grass along the fence?"

Leaning over, he parted the grass. There was a nest on the ground that sheltered little birds with tiny black eyes.

"Partridges," said Pierce. "Don't ever bother these eggs. We want them to grow up so we can hunt them in the fall."

Hattie remembered the baby chicks she had let die, but she didn't think Pierce did.

Trudging along on the dusty path, Hattie's thoughts again turned to the heat. She reached up to swipe her bangs from her sweaty forehead. There wasn't even a little breeze to cool her.

Ahead she saw the windmill. Hattie knew it was used to pump water into a large tank from which the cows drank. The tank was brimming full of cool water.

"Pierce, I have an idea," Hattie began.

"Stop," said Pierce. "Don't even whisper it. You'll only get us in trouble."

"This is a good idea." Hattie paused. "Don't you feel hot and sweaty?"

"Well, yes I do," said Pierce.

"Then let's jump into the tank and cool off," Hattie pleaded.

"That's a crazy idea, Hattie," insisted Pierce. "You know the cattle won't drink the water after we've splashed around in there. We'll stir up the green algae on the bottom of the tank. That will stir up Dad, if he catches us! Don't you remember? Dad said we had to hurry back and not loiter along the way."

"Well, I'm so hot, I feel like I'll die if I don't cool off," Hattie retorted. "I'm sure Dad wouldn't want to find me dead out in the pasture. I'm going for a swim, even if you're not!"

"Well, go ahead," Pierce said. "I'll have no part of your scheme. Just remember what I told you—Dad is not going to like it."

"Dad won't have to know," replied Hattie. But Pierce had turned to get the cows and didn't hear her.

As fast as she could, Hattie made her way to the tank. How cool and refreshing the water looked! She stood gazing at it. If she jumped in with her clothes on, Dad would surely know what she had done.

"I'll just have to go in without my clothes," declared Hattie. Quickly she stripped to her petticoat, and with a big splash she jumped in the water.

What a heavenly feeling it was! Hattie pretended she was in the ocean, floating around and around, with one hand safely on the edge of the tank. Then she pretended she was kidnapped, dumped overboard, and waiting for someone to rescue her. Suddenly Hattie thought of a poem:

> *I wonder who the prince will be*
> *Who will come to rescue me?*
> *I hope he comes before I drown*
> *And carries me back to town.*

Time was slipping away. Pierce had already headed back to the barn with the cows. The sun was setting, and the air was turning cool. Stopping her daydreams, Hattie jumped out of the tank. That's when she noticed someone coming down the path toward her.

And it wasn't a prince. It was Dad! In his hand he had a fly swatter, the rubber one with holes in it. That meant only one thing—a spanking!

Hattie tried desperately to get into her clothes, but her slip was sopping wet and the clothes stuck to her as she tried to pull them on.

"Hattie, Hattie! How many times have I told you to stay out of that tank!" Dad scolded. "Here you are, swimming in your petticoat!" With that, Dad gave Hattie two good swats on her back side.

"Ouch!" Hattie wailed. "That hurt!"

"I meant it to hurt," said Dad. "Maybe next time you will obey."

Big tears came to her eyes as Dad started back down the lane to the house. While Hattie finished getting back into her clothes, she thought over what she had done.

Feeling sorry and ashamed, Hattie ran to catch up with Dad. "I'm sorry, Dad. I'll never, do it again."

Dad took her hand and they walked side by side. "Hattie, *liefheid,* if you don't learn to obey as a child, you are surely going to disappoint God as an adult. I only spanked you because I love you."

Hattie rubbed her bottom; it was still smarting. Right at that moment, she wished Dad didn't love her quite so much!

Chapter 8

High Over Iowa

*O*ne day in the middle of summer, the air was stifling hot all day. Big, black clouds suddenly appeared in the late afternoon. The air was heavy and it was hard to breathe. The wind began to whirl the dirt around the yard and to make the trees rustle.

Hattie, Clarence, and Leona were playing hopscotch on the front walk.

"Storm's coming," Dad said. He stood in the yard, looking at the fast-moving clouds. "We'd better put everything away."

"Will it be a bad storm?" asked Hattie. She didn't mind if it rained and cooled things off, but she didn't like bad storms. Bad storms made roofs blow off and ruined gardens.

"I can't tell," said Dad. "We'd better be ready, just in case. All you children get your things and go inside."

Suddenly Dad heard the sound of an engine

getting louder and louder. He looked up. Coming right down toward them was an airplane. Flying lower and lower, the plane was landing at the end of the field next to the house.

"Look," said Dad, "he's spinning the airplane around so that the tail is facing the direction of the wind."

"I think he shut off the engine. He's climbing out of the cockpit," added Clarence.

"Let's go see him," Hattie said, and all the children ran toward the parked airplane. They saw the pilot jump out of the cockpit and open the luggage compartment.

"Can I help you?" called Dad, as they came close to the plane.

"Yes, we need to use these stakes and ropes to tie down the airplane before the storm sets in," said the pilot.

"We don't have much time," said Dad. He looked anxiously at the clouds churning overhead. He helped the pilot pound the stakes in the ground. Then they tied the ropes from the stakes to the airplane to make it secure.

"Now all I need to do is snap these canvas covers over the cockpit," said the pilot.

"We just finished in time," said Dad. He felt a blast of wind with dust and leaves flying through the air. Picking up Leona, Dad yelled, "Let's get out of this weather and run for the house."

Mom and Kathryn were watching for them on the front porch.

"Won't you have a cup of coffee with us?" Mom invited the pilot. He smiled and nodded. He was glad to sit down at the table and rest.

"My name is Hank Summers," he said. "I came from Mason City. A few of us pilots were in an air show. I was on my way to another air show in South Dakota."

The family listened eagerly as the pilot told them he had been a flight pilot in World War I, and had been in combat duty.

"Now I'm part of a group called the Iowa Air Circus," he said.

"How can you have a circus in the air?" asked Clarence.

"We do all kinds of acrobatics," laughed Mr. Summers. "We even have wing-walkers, people who climb out on the wings while the plane is in the air."

"How come they don't fall off?" asked Leona.

"They're tied down pretty securely so they can't fall," said the pilot.

"I've read about those wing-walkers. Some people call them daredevils," said Mr. Hart.

"Crowds usually like the end of the show best," continued the pilot. "That's when we offer rides. Folks stand in line to buy tickets, and then wait for their turn to go up in the airplane."

"How many can you take in your plane at one time?" asked Hattie. She was fascinated and just wanted him to keep talking.

"Maybe you noticed my plane has two cockpits," said the pilot. "I ride in the back one, and the front one is for passengers—two at a time."

Hattie felt like she was in a storybook that had come to life.

Just as quickly as the rain had begun, it stopped and Mr. Summers stood up.

"I had better see if any damage has been done to the plane," said the pilot. "If not, I'll be on my way to Sioux Falls. Thanks for taking me in out of the rain."

The whole Hart family went with Mr. Summers to look at his plane. "Well, I'm lucky. It looks pretty good," he said. "I do have one problem—I have to stand and pull the propellor to start the engine. I need someone inside the plane at the same time to turn the switch and crank the throttle."

It sounded complicated to Hattie, but not to Dad. He had started enough Model T cars to know what the man was talking about.

"I can do that for you," said Dad as he climbed in the cockpit. The two men soon had the engine roaring.

Before Mr. Summers climbed into the rear seat, he shouted, "Why don't you stay in that seat, Mr. Hart.

Why did I ever get in this Airplane? she asked herself.

Maybe one of your children would like to come along with you for an airplane ride." Then he turned to the children. "Which one of you wants to go for a ride?"

All of them started to back away, as if to say, "Not me, not me." Hattie was scared too, but she had just been dreaming about flying over the jungles of Africa. Suddenly she felt brave.

"I'll go," she said and climbed in next to her father. When they were safely strapped in, the pilot put on his helmet and goggles, and started to taxi the plane down the field. With a blast from the engine, the plane roared up and away.

All of a sudden Hattie remembered she had always been afraid of heights. And she was higher than she had ever been, even at the fair! She closed her eyes and leaned back. *Oh, I wish I was back on the ground. Why did I ever get in this airplane*, she asked herself.

"Look," Dad yelled over the noise of the plane, "there's the town of Harris. There's the church, and there's the school. Hattie, do you see Ruthie's house? And look, the sandpit and there's the creek and the pasture pond." Dad was really enjoying his ride.

Hattie didn't say a word.

When they were safe on the ground, Leona asked, "Hattie, were you scared?"

"No," she said, tossing her hair and looking up at the sky. She didn't say that after they were in the air, she never—even once—opened her eyes.

60

Chapter 9

Whoa, Topsy!

*H*attie made a space for her sister next to her favorite doll. "You may sit next to Loretta Lavender," she said.

"Why can't I sit next to Maybelle?" said Leona. "She's my doll."

"Because," said Hattie, "when you're invited to a party, you sit where the hostess seats you."

Hattie still liked to play dolls with Leona even though most of her friends didn't play with them anymore. She was so wrapped up in her play, Mom had to call her twice to get her attention.

"Do you know where Clarence and Pierce are?" asked Mom.

"I saw them riding on Topsy, going toward Bests' farm," Hattie answered.

Topsy had been a race horse, and had won prizes in the harness races at the county fair. Dad bought Topsy at an auction for a low price because she was getting old but she had not been trained to pull a plow. He was delighted to own such a fast horse. "When I hitch her to the buggy she gets me to town and back in almost no time at all," he said.

Pierce and Clarence had found another use for Topsy. "Boy, can she go fast when we ride her bareback," Pierce said, flinging his arm to show just how fast. Pierce and Clarence were always glad for an excuse to take Topsy.

"Hattie," said Mom, "would you please walk down to the Bests and tell the boys to bring Topsy home? Dad needs her for a trip to town."

"I'll be right back," Hattie told Leona and the others at her tea party. "Wait for me."

When Hattie reached the Bests' farm, her brothers were playing ball and didn't want to quit.

"Why don't you take Topsy home?" said Pierce. He knew Topsy might give Hattie a fast ride, but it wouldn't hurt her. Besides Hattie had surprised him with a few tricks herself.

"There's nothing to it," said Pierce. "She's as gentle as old Betsy. You'll have fun riding her home."

Hattie paused. She had never ridden Topsy before. She could lead the horse home, but it would be more exciting to ride.

"I'll do it!" she told Pierce.

Riding Topsy by herself made Hattie feel very grownup. Pierce and Clarence snickered, knowing Hattie was in for a fast ride.

Pierce helped Hattie mount Topsy and handed her the reins.

"Okay, Topsy," said Hattie. "Here we go." She gave a couple of clicks with her tongue, and Topsy walked down the driveway toward the road.

Pierce watched Hattie. "Looks like she is doing all right," he said. But just as he was about to pick up the ball again, he noticed the horse break into a trot— and a car was coming. "Uh-oh, Clarence," he said. "Maybe we better help her."

Hattie had grabbed Topsy's mane with one hand and was pulling on the reins with the other. "Wait a minute," said Hattie. "Don't go so fast!"

But Topsy had no intention of slowing down.

The car came right up behind Hattie, who was riding in the middle of the road. "Ka-ooga! ka-ooga!" The car's horn blasted to let Hattie know they wanted to pass.

Topsy had learned as a racehorse not to let anything or anyone pass her. Away she went, full speed, leaving the car behind.

Hattie was terrified. "Stop Topsy, STOP!" she yelled. But Topsy went faster than ever. Hattie clenched both her arms around the horse's neck. Tears of fright came to her eyes.

"WHOA, TOPSY!" she screamed.

Topsy was almost to the Hart yard. *She's got to slow down to turn into the driveway*, thought Hattie, who was now crying hard.

But Topsy didn't slow down. She raced full speed

ahead for the barnyard, chickens flying in all directions before her.

Hattie knew she would either crash through the gate or jump over it. She closed her eyes, expecting the worst.

At the last second, Topsy put out her legs stiffly in front of her and slid to a very sudden stop.

Hattie somersaulted right over Topsy's head and landed with a thud on her back—just a foot short of the gate.

Pierce and Clarence had been running after Topsy and her rider as fast as they could the whole way home. When they came to the yard, they saw Topsy standing at the barn gate and Hattie lying motionless on the ground.

Hattie was stunned. She heard Pierce and Clarence coming, but her eyes were still closed. *My dumb brothers! I'll make them sorry they ever put me on that horse*, she thought. She lay very still and pretended the fall had knocked her out.

"Maybe she's dead," said Clarence.

"I think she's still breathing," said Pierce, ready to cry. "We should never have put her on that horse. We better carry her inside to Mom."

"What are you going to tell Mom?" said Clarence. "It was your idea to put her on the horse."

Carefully they lifted Hattie's limp body and carried her across the yard to the house. They struggled up the porch steps, and laid her on the sofa in the parlor.

The boys, both crying, ran up the stairs, "Mom, Mom! Hattie's hurt real bad. She may be dying."

Hattie stretched her arms and legs. They seemed okay, although her head hurt a little.

Within seconds, Clarence and Pierce were coming downstairs again, with Mom hurrying behind them.

There sat Hattie on the couch, as if nothing had happened.

"Why is everyone crying?" Hattie asked casually.

"We thought you were dead," said Clarence. "You were just faking."

"You scared us to death," said Pierce.

"Serves you right," said Hattie, "for putting me on that horse."

Pierce and Clarence hung their heads.

"What about that, boys?" Mom asked. "You knew that horse ran too fast. It's not enough for me to lose Kathryn—"

"What do you mean, Mom, 'lose Kathryn'?" Hattie quickly asked.

"Oh, Oh—I must have said the wrong thing." Mom turned quickly and went back upstairs.

Hattie and her brothers looked at one another. *What's going on?* Hattie thought.

Chapter 10

Lost at the Lake

*I*t was a rare summer day with warm sun, a fresh breeze, and no pressing work to do. Dad volunteered to take Hattie, Clarence, Leona, and Ervin, to Lake Okabena, just over the Iowa border in Worthington, Minnesota.

"The in-between children sometimes get neglected," he told Mom. "If Hattie promises to take care of Ervin, I think I can manage."

"I promise! I promise!" said Hattie. She would have promised anything at that moment. "I'll never take my eyes off Ervin."

Everyone scurried to get ready.

"Don't take the best towels," directed Mom.

"Hattie's a pig. She took the biggest one," Clarence tattled.

"I'm going to share it with Ervin," replied Hattie. "Mom, if I wear my oldest dress, can I go into the water?" Hattie begged. "I'll take some dry clothes along."

"I want to go in the water too," said Clarence.

"Me too," said Leona.

"It's still too cold. I think it will be enough just to wade in the water," said Mom.

"Close to the shore," added Dad.

Clarence insisted that he take along his fishing rod. Actually, it was only a stick with a string and hook on the end. Dad put tape over the hook so it wouldn't stick anyone on the way to the lake. Hattie decided to take a book along to read while she was taking care of little Ervin. She knew he wouldn't go near the water.

Oh, well, it will be fun anyway, thought Hattie. Maybe Dad will keep an eye on Ervin part of the time.

Everyone climbed into the car—never suspecting what the outcome would be.

The blue sky was cloudless when they arrived. A bright sun warmed the sand and the lake. Hattie found a place on the sand to spread out her towel, and Dad spread an old quilt nearby. Clarence grabbed his fishing pole as Leona ran into the water, splashing carelessly.

"I bet I'll catch more fish than you could ever catch," said Clarence.

"Don't be so sure," said Hattie. "Remember when we went fishing in the creek with Katrina? Who caught the most bullheads then?" challenged Hattie.

Clarence didn't like to be reminded of that. His total catch had been zero. Hattie and Katrina had each caught six good-sized fish, enough for Mom to fry for supper for the whole family.

"I betcha a quarter I can catch more fish than you." challenged Clarence. He had heard Pierce and his friends say, "betcha a quarter," and he had earned a quarter weeding Mrs. Best's garden.

Hattie thought that was a fine bargain—but Dad put a stop to it.

"No gambling . . . the Bible says. . ." mumbled Dad, half asleep under a newspaper that shaded his eyes from the hot sun.

Hattie started reading her library book, *Aladdin's Lamp.* Ervin kept busy picking up little pebbles around the edge of the blanket and giving them to Hattie. All the time Hattie was reading, she could hear Leona splashing in the water.

Why am I reading on such a beautiful day when I could be playing in the water? she thought. *Maybe I can get Ervin busy building a castle of pebbles and can get away for a little while.*

"Here, Ervin, see how many little stones you can put together on the towel," she said as she handed him a small handful of stones. "But don't leave the towel. Stay here with Dad."

"Stay wif Dad," he said, already busy putting one pebble on top of another.

With that promise, Hattie ran to join Leona, calling to Dad as she left, "Please watch Ervin!"

Hattie loved the feel of the water on her bare feet. She stood on one foot and waved the other one back and forth making patterns in the water. Then she waded farther into the water, and let the edge of her dress float out around her. Hattie thought it looked like the petals on a flower. "I'm a water lily," she imagined.

After some time, Hattie remembered she should check on her little brother. As she came out of the water, she noticed at once that Ervin had left the towel and was nowhere in sight.

"Where is Ervin?" she asked, shaking Dad awake.

"I don't know," Dad said as he removed the newspapers from his eyes. "I thought you were watching him. I fell asleep."

Hattie's stomach did an uneasy flip as she realized that Dad had never heard her ask him to watch little Ervin.

"We'll just have to search for him," said Dad. "He couldn't have gone far with his short little legs."

Dad's words reassured Hattie, but after the family had been looking for several minutes, they were all alarmed.

"Look at those trees along the shore," Clarence said. "Maybe he's hiding behind one of those."

"Maybe he's dead!" wailed Leona.

"We have to keep looking until we find him," Dad said. Then he called as loudly as he could:

"Ervin! Ervin! Where are you?"

Clarence yelled even louder. "Ervin! Ervin! Don't worry, we'll find you!"

Hattie said nothing. She felt sick. She had promised to watch her brother and then she had left him. "Dear God," she prayed silently. "Don't let him be drowned. Don't let him be kidnapped! Let us find him. Please don't let him be dead!"

Again they all called, "Ervin! Ervin!"

After more minutes of looking, calling, and walking, Dad said, "Let's go back to the car. We have to get the police to help us find him. It will soon be dark and we won't be able to see anything."

They all headed to the car. Hattie ran in front of the others. Reaching the edge of the lake, she looked down at the water and whispered, "Oh, please, God, don't let us find him floating in the water or lying on the bottom of the lake."

Turning around, she saw an outdoor toilet near the shore. Hattie realized she had to make a stop there. She couldn't possibly wait until she got home. By now, Hattie was crying so hard, she could hardly see. She dashed in the building and stopped in wonder. There on the floor was little Ervin, fast asleep!

"Dad! Dad!" screamed Hattie. "I found him! I did! I found him!" She half-carried, half-dragged the sleepy toddler to her father's waiting arms.

"Let's get down on our knees and thank God," said

71

Clarence yelled even louder, "Ervin! Ervin!
Don't worry; we'll find you!"

Dad with tears streaming down his cheeks. He hadn't scolded Hattie for not watching Ervin because he felt so guilty himself for not keeping an eye on the little boy.

Few words, but many tears, flowed while the Harts thanked God, kneeling on the sandy stretch of shore. As they climbed in the car and headed home, Hattie thought, *God had been good!*

Chapter 11

A Trip to Sioux City

*H*attie listened to the rhythmic clatter of the train as it rolled over the tracks. She still could barely believe that Mom and Dad had given her permission to visit her cousin Hilda in Sioux City, Iowa.

"This is my only chance to visit her this summer," Hattie had pleaded. "School has already started in Sioux City."

"Well, she did invite you," said Dad . "It is a good way to get to know your cousin better."

Hattie could tell her father was weakening.

"Hattie always seems to get into so much trouble here at home," said Mom. "Who knows what might happen if she were out of my sight!"

"Mom, I was only trouble when I was younger," Hattie protested. "I'm not a baby anymore."

Mom and Dad looked at one another with a smile. "All right, Hattie, we're trusting you," Dad had said. "We want you to be a proper young lady. Do exactly what your Uncle Sip and Aunt Rica tell you, and if you have any ideas, ask your aunt or uncle about them first."

Hilda's mother, Aunt Rica, was one of Hattie's favorite aunts, and it was always fun to visit Hilda. Aunt Rica really liked children. She had seven of her own.

Mom let Hattie wear her green calico dress on the train. Usually, she wore it only on Sundays. She had polished her shoes the night before until they looked like new.

Hattie leaned her head back against the seat. *I can't believe I'm on the way to Sioux City*, she thought.

The conductor tapped her on the shoulder. "The next town will be your stop."

She looked out the window. Everything looked much like it did back home. There were lots of flat fields and not many houses. The train was slowing down as the whistle blew and soon it stopped.

"Hattie! Hattie! Here we are!" beamed a voice from the station platform. Hilda ran to greet Hattie. "You've grown a lot taller since the last time I saw you."

Hattie was glad she didn't say, "and skinnier."

Uncle Sip picked up Hattie's boxy suitcase and put it on the wagon. Hattie and Hilda chattered together until they turned off the gravel road to Uncle Sip's farmyard. Hattie stared at a weather-beaten square house with several tall trees that leaned against it as if to keep it from falling over.

"Will there be room for all of us?" asked Hattie.

"Oh, that's not our house," said Hilda. "That's where we keep the chickens." Hattie was relieved.

"That's our home," said Uncle Sip, proudly pointing to a frame two-story building. Most of the paint had disappeared, but the house was big and looked sturdy. Uncle Sip helped the girls down from the wagon.

Out of the house tumbled one, two, three, four, five, six children, and Aunt Rica. The children, of all ages and sizes, were squealing with delight that a visitor had come to play with them. The warm welcome reminded Hattie of home.

"We are so glad you're here," said Aunt Rica. "Hilda has prayed for days that nothing would keep you from coming." Hattie felt as comfortable with Hilda's family as with her own family.

Uncle Sip took Hattie's suitcase to Hilda's room. The room wasn't as fancy as Hattie's room back home. It had a linoleum floor and a painted-white iron bed big enough for two people. In one corner was a round black stovepipe that came from the kitchen and went through the ceiling. When the weather was cold, this pipe brought a little heat to the room.

"Do you like the nice coverlet Mother made because you were coming?" asked Hilda.

"It's a beautiful rose color," said Hattie as she stroked the soft bedspread.

Hilda helped Hattie unpack her suitcase before supper. Hattie felt like she was at home with her mom and dad and all the children around the table. The family laughed and talked a lot. Aunt Rica served one of Hattie's favorite dishes—soup'n brie. Hattie poured thickened buttermilk on her plate and decorated it with syrup she poured from a pretty pitcher.

Aunt Rica smiled at Hattie. "The children like to pour syrup in the shape of a letter, Hattie. There is only enough syrup to make your first initial."

Hattie noticed that her older cousin William used a lot of syrup, but his name started with a W. Hattie remembered that her mother had told her to be a proper lady, so she didn't say anything.

Right after supper it was Hilda's bedtime.

"Can't we stay up late because Hattie is here?" asked Hilda.

"Hattie is probably tired from her train ride," said Aunt Rica. "And tomorrow will come soon enough. You have to be up bright and early to get to school on time."

The next morning, Uncle Sip took the girls to school in the wagon. The school was only a mile from their home and Hilda and the other children usually walked. Today was special because Hattie was visiting.

Hilda's school was very different from Hattie's. All the grades were together in one room. Hattie came in the school through a cloakroom that stretched across the front of the building. A long row of metal coat hooks paraded down one wall, and a bucket of drinking water with a dipper sat on a table in the corner. When she opened the door to the classroom, she smelled chalk dust and varnish, just like her school.

Hattie pointed to the rows of desks. "How do you know where to sit if all the grades are in one room?" she asked.

"The little kids sit at the front desks and the older ones sit in the back," replied Hilda. "Here they come now."

Soon the room was filled with students. After the pledge of allegiance to the flag, Miss Reimer, the teacher, announced that she had a surprise for the class.

"You may wonder what the syrup pail is doing on the piano," she told the class. "It's full of cream."

"I don't like cream," said a small girl in the front row.

"We aren't going to drink it," laughed Miss Reimer. "I've been letting it thicken for several days, and today is the day we are going to make butter. Isn't that special?" Miss Reimer had not grown up on a farm, and making butter was a novelty to her.

"My ma just makes butter by shaking a can of

cream up and down," said one of the younger boys.

"Yes, but do you know why?" asked the teacher. "We'll talk about that after recess." She assigned the older children to write a short essay on the various uses of butter. Those in the middle grades had to think up different words that described butter. The younger children were to draw pictures that made them think of butter. To inspire their drawings, she held up several pictures.

I'll bet it's tricky, thought Hattie, *to keep everyone busy.* Some were finished sooner than others. Miss Reimer seemed glad when recess came.

"Hilda, would you and your friend do me a favor and erase the blackboard?" asked the teacher. "I need to go outside to watch the children."

Hattie was glad to help. It made her feel important.

"These erasers are impossible!" said Hilda. "I'm going outside to clean them."

Hattie knew that meant pounding them together until they were free of chalk dust. While Hilda was gone, Hattie walked to the window and watched the kids playing.

Why does Miss Reimer think making butter is so interesting? Hattie said to herself. *I've helped Mom make butter lots of times.* Hattie carefully picked up the pail filled with cream. *Wouldn't Miss Reimer be surprised if I had the butter all made when the children come in from recess?* Hattie took the pail and shook it up and down as hard as she could.

Hilda came back into the room. "What are you doing?" she asked.

"Making butter," said Hattie. "Do you want to help?"

"Sure," Hilda replied, and she took a turn shaking the pail. Suddenly the lid flew off and clabbered cream splashed all over the room, the floor, and some of the desks.

"Oh, no!" said Hattie. "Look what we've done!"

"Miss Reimer is going to be mad," declared Hilda. "She's been talking about making butter for days—and she's been waiting for that cream to be ready all week."

"We have to get out of here before she comes back!" said Hattie. She grabbed her coat and ran out the back door with Hilda following her.

They ran until they were out of breath. Before they reached Hilda's house, they stopped.

"We can't go home," said Hilda. "Mother will wonder why we're home so early."

"Let's hide in the bushes until school is over," suggested Hattie. "Then we can go in."

It seemed like forever before they heard the bell ring at the school. Soon the other children came home, and Hattie and Hilda went in the house trying to look innocent, but fearing the worst.

Aunt Rica asked knowingly, "Where have you

been? Miss Reimer called and said you weren't in school this afternoon. She also told me what happened."

Hattie knew that their sins had found them out.

"I never meant for the lid to fly off," sniffed Hilda.

"It was all my fault," said Hattie solemnly. "I started it."

"It was bad enough to meddle with the teacher's things," said Aunt Rica sternly, "but it was worse for you to run away. You two had better march right back to school and help Miss Reimer in any way you can. You made a lot of extra work for her."

Hattie and Hilda agreed. When they got back to the school, Miss Reimer was on her hands and knees, scrubbing the floor.

"Please forgive us!" said Hilda.

"We shouldn't have touched your things and we shouldn't have run away," added Hattie.

"Is it too late for us to help?" asked Hilda.

"I know you didn't mean to do it. It was an accident," said Miss Reimer, "but I would be glad for some help rinsing this floor."

Hattie thought Hilda was lucky to have Miss Reimer for a teacher. *I'm pretty lucky too,* she realized suddenly. *Aunt Rica could have sent me right back on the train!*

Chapter 12

Red Hands for All

om called up the stairs. "Hattie, I need you to make the beds and dust. When you're finished, I can use some help in the parlor and dining room."

"That's Kathryn's job," said Hattie.

"Kathryn went to Worthington to shop for some new clothes," said Mom.

"More new clothes?" Hattie said in surprise. "She's got twice as many as I have already!"

"Never mind about Kathryn," said Mom. "Just get busy. Lawrence is coming over for supper, and I'm sure Kathryn wants the house clean."

"He's here every night," said Hattie. "I'm getting tired of having him around so much."

"He only comes on Friday nights and Sunday after church, and that's not every night," said Mom.

"It sure seems like it," muttered Hattie as she ran up the stairs.

She really didn't mind that Lawrence Van Wyck

came over a lot. She was glad that her sister had a boyfriend. Actually she just didn't like having to do Kathryn's housework.

I think I'll do my room first, Hattie thought. She started to make her bed, and then she noticed *Black Beauty* under her pillow. She had read until late the night before, and she was at the best part.

Hattie picked up the book and started reading. An hour passed and Hattie was still reading.

"Hattie!" called Mom from downstairs, "Are you finished yet?"

Hattie had taken her shoes off when she lay on the bed to read. Tap, tap, tap went her shoes, not with her feet in them, but her hands! She wanted Mom to think she was working.

Hattie read a few more pages before she tossed the covers up on the bed and raced down the stairs. Lawrence was already there. *Oh dear*, thought Hattie, *I shouldn't have read so long.*

Minutes later, Kathryn arrived home. She whisked off her coat. "Do you like it?" She smiled and twirled around in her new silk dress of pink-and-blue checks with a lace collar.

It's beautiful, thought Hattie. *But why is Kathryn so dressed up? Even her hair is freshly waved.*

Hattie looked at the table, all set with Mom's best white dishes for twelve.

"What's going on here?" asked Hattie.

"Let's all sit down and eat supper. Then you'll find out," said Dad.

After the blessing, Dad cleared his throat. "I have an announcement to make. Lawrence has asked Kathryn to marry him. Kathryn has accepted his proposal, and Mom and I have given our blessing."

Hattie was stunned. She knew Lawrence and Kathryn liked each other, but she never wanted to believe they would actually get married.

"Our family will never be the same without Kathryn," said Hattie sadly. "She's only seventeen."

"Cheer up. This is supposed to be good news," said Pierce.

"When are you getting married?" asked Leona.

"This coming September," replied Lawrence.

"Can we all go to the wedding?" asked Clarence.

"We wouldn't want you to miss it," laughed Kathryn.

"Is the wedding going to be at the church?" asked Pierce.

"No, Kathryn wants to be married right here in our house," said Mom proudly.

Hattie couldn't believe it. Her older sister would be leaving. She decided if everyone else was so pleased about the wedding, she would try to be happy too.

"Dad, what about the square dance that Pierce wanted to have on Labor Day?" Hattie asked. "Can we have one to celebrate Kathryn's wedding?"

"Well, maybe we can. You'll have to help Mom. She's going to have a lot to do with the wedding."

"I can help," volunteered Leona.

"I don't think it will take us long to get ready," said Hattie. "When I work, I work really fast."

"I know," Mom said. "I heard you running upstairs to finish your chores."

Hattie looked down at her plate, but she didn't say anything.

"I would love to have a square dance," said Kathryn, "if it isn't too much trouble for everyone."

"Kathryn, you've never been too much trouble and that's a fact," said Dad.

The day of the square dance Hattie was sitting on her bed. She picked up a pencil and her writing pad. Today, more than any other day, she wished she could be Kathryn, getting all the attention and acting like a princess at a ball.

Quickly, she wrote a poem to her sister and called it "Ode to Kathryn."

> *You know what I'd like*
> *I'd like to be you*
> *For just one week*
> *Or maybe two.*
> *Then I'd do what you do*
> *And go where you go*
> *And hear Mom say, "Hattie,*
> *You're my pet, you know."*

Knowing there was work to be done before everyone arrived, Hattie put her pad away and scurried downstairs, wondering if she would always be jealous of Kathryn.

Her sister's brown eyes sparkled as she said to Mom, "I'm so happy you and Dad are letting me have this party."

"I wish I were getting married. Then I could have a party," Hattie said sadly.

"You're invited to my party," said Kathryn as she swirled around the room in a pretty new blue dress.

"Who's coming?" asked Hattie, suddenly interested. "Besides relatives?"

"Everybody from the Young People's Society at church, Mrs. Best and Arnold, and some of your friends from church may come. I think the Koostras are coming. Of course, the Van Wycks."

The Van Wycks. Kathryn's future in-laws! thought Hattie.

Mom broke Hattie's train of thought. "Get busy, Hattie, and make some more sandwiches. The company will be here soon."

Mom had made potato salad and gelatin the night before, and she had baked Kathryn's favorite cake— an angel food cake with white frosting and colored sugar on top. Hattie wished the cake were chocolate with dark chocolate frosting. That was *her* favorite!

As soon as most of the company had arrived, Dad

gave the blessing. Some of the people from church had also brought food, so there was plenty for everyone. Hattie noticed later that Kathryn and Lawrence were sitting on the porch swing eating their food.

Hattie rolled her eyes. "It's a good thing I don't have to sit with a boyfriend. I would never get to talk with anyone else."

Mom was cutting the cake. Everybody was congratulating Kathryn and telling her how pretty she looked. When Kathryn blushed, her cheeks looked rosy and her whole face lit up. *I wish everyone was here to see me*, thought Hattie, *and I wish I was as beautiful as Kathryn.*

Hattie heard the fiddler tuning his fiddle. It was square dance time on the front lawn!

Soon everyone was either dancing to the the music, or clapping their hands and watching the young people swing their partners. The weather was just right for square dancing—not too hot nor too cold.

They danced until it was too dark to see. Hattie wished it could have lasted forever.

When all the guests where gone, Hattie and Kathryn went to the kitchen to do the dishes. Kathryn usually washed while Hattie wiped.

Hattie noticed how red and chapped Kathryn's hands were.

Still jealous of how pretty Kathryn looked, Hattie

decided to tease her about her red hands.

"Your hands look like lobster claws," laughed Hattie. "What does Lawrence think when you're holding hands? Look at mine." She held up her hands for Kathryn to see.

Kathryn didn't say anything for a few moments. Then she remembered last Sunday's sermon.

"I'd be worried if I had white hands like that. You might have leprosy!"

"Leprosy?" Hattie also remembered the pastor's sermon. She looked at her hands again. "I don't think I have leprosy," she said, trying to sound bold. "If I do have it, what should I do?"

"Get your hands in soapy water as soon as you can. You can begin right now by washing these dishes. Every chance you have, put your hands in hot, soapy water." Kathryn's eyes twinkled.

Hattie took her sister's words seriously. She washed the dishes, laundered the clothes, and scrubbed the floors. Pretty soon, her hands looked like Kathryn's—red and raw.

"Why are you suddenly doing all the washing chores?" Mom asked in a few days. "I miss your help taking care of the children."

"I don't want to have leprosy," Hattie explained.

"Leprosy!" said Mom. "What do you mean?"

"Kathryn said I'd get leprosy if I didn't keep my hands in hot, soapy water," Hattie said.

Mom laughed. "Ya, Hattie, you have been fooled. Kathryn tricked you so you would do her work!"

Hattie couldn't believe it. She had been so foolish. Maybe it was time for Kathryn to leave home after all!

Chapter 13

Kathryn's Wedding

*K*athryn's wedding was only a few weeks away. The Hart house had been cleaned from top to bottom. Floors were washed and waxed. Windows were cleaned until they sparkled. Curtains were laundered, starched, and ironed. There was so much to do, Mom was glad when the neighbors volunteered to bring in food and bake the wedding cake.

The day before the wedding, Beattie, Hattie's good friend from church, came to help Hattie decorate the parlor. Kathryn and Lawrence were to be married there.

"Let's make a beautiful arch for them to stand under," said Hattie. "We can use pink and blue crepe paper."

Hattie and Beattie worked hard. They cut crepe paper into strips and hung streamers over the door frame.

"Isn't it beautiful?" said Hattie as she stood back

and admired it.

The day of the wedding was a beautiful fall day. Upstairs Hattie helped Kathryn dress. Her wedding gown was made of blue silk with a white lace collar and cuffs and a row of silver buttons down the front. It was long with a ruffle at the bottom. Only the toes of Kathryn's patent leather slippers showed.

"Here's your bouquet," said Hattie. She pulled one of the little white garden mums from the bouquet and pinned it in Kathryn's hair.

Suddenly Kathryn kissed Hattie on the cheek. "I'll miss you, Hattie," she said.

"I'll miss you too, especially when I have to do the dishes." Hattie smiled as she turned to go downstairs.

As Kathryn walked down the stairs, the pianist had already started playing wedding music. The wedding was small—just the two families. There wasn't room for anyone else.

Hattie looked at Kathryn and Lawrence standing in the doorway under the beautifully decorated arch. Suddenly Hattie started to cry.

Mom, seeing Hattie, started to cry herself. It wasn't long before Leona was crying, too.

The minister took his place and began the ceremony. Hattie blinked back her tears. Dad looked so proud standing beside Kathryn. Kathryn said her vows softly, and Hattie could barely hear Lawrence at all. Before Hattie was ready for it, the minister was introducing Mr. and Mrs. Lawrence Van Wyck.

Everyone hugged and kissed the bride.

"Throw your bouquet over your shoulder," said Hattie. "The one who catches it will be married next."

Kathryn went halfway up the stairs and threw her bouquet high in the air. Clarence reached for it and caught it.

"You're not supposed to catch it," said Leona. "You're a boy." And she grabbed it out of his hands. Everyone laughed.

Suddenly there was a knock at the door. Hattie ran to answer it.

It was the delivery boy from the grocery. "Here's the ice cream Mrs. Hart ordered for Mrs. Van Wyck."

How strange, thought Hattie, *Why is Lawrence's mother getting something at our house.* "I'm not sure this is supposed to come here," said Hattie.

"Oh, yes, it is, " said Mom as she came to the door. "It's for Kathryn."

That's right! Mrs. Van Wyck! thought Hattie. Everything about Kathryn would be different now— even her name.

It was time to cut the wedding cake, but Hattie noticed someone had already gotten to the cake— Ervin had pulled himself up to the cake plate and left a handprint on one side.

"I'll just turn the cake around," said Hattie. "Then they won't see where Ervin messed it up."

Quickly, Hattie got her box camera.

After the cake and ice cream were served, Kathryn and Lawrence went outside. Quickly Hattie got her box camera to take a picture of the couple standing in the yard. Then Lawrence and Kathryn left for their honeymoon.

The house was suddenly very quiet. Dad put his arm around Mom, something he seldom did in public. "Our firstborn has left the nest," he said.

"I hope they are happy," said Mom.

Hattie could see tears in her mother's eyes, but Hattie didn't want to be sad again. Maybe if she said something funny, it would help. "I'll bet you won't cry when I get married. You'll be glad to get rid of me."

Dad looked thoughtful. "Don't leave for a long, long time," he said. "I need my little Hattie around."

Tears came to Hattie's eyes again. But this time she was happy.

Experience the *Treasures of Childhood*
Growing up in a twelve-member family on a farm in the 1920s creates many opportunities for adventure and discovery. Enjoy each exciting book in the *Treasures of Childhood* series as young Hattie Hart explores the magnificent world around her and learns important value lessons in the process.

Meet Hattie
Hattie has a difficult time obeying the simple rules on her family's farm. Whether she's stretching the truth to sell seeds or breaking Mom's best candy dish, each new day teaches her the value her family's love.

Hattie's Holidays
Hattie sneaks out of the house on her birthday to try out her new skates—and breaks her ankle! Then, she lights a candle and accidentally sets the Christmas tree on fire. Through these experiences, Hattie learns the hard way that rules are not to spoil her fun, but to protect her.

Hattie's Adventures
Her best friend gets stranded on the roof when Hattie and her brothers take away the ladder she used to get up. Then, Hattie thinks up a dirty trick to get even with her brother for a prank he pulled on her. Through all the teasing and adventure, they learn to laugh together and appreciate each other.

All titles are available at your favorite Christian bookstore.